Porridge the Tartan Cat

To the special grown ups in my life, who
helped a small kid think big. Me-thanks! – A.D.

To my ever caring and supportive hubby Colin – Y.S.

Young Kelpies is an imprint of Floris Books
First published in 2017 by Floris Books
Text © 2017 Alan Dapré. Illustrations © 2017 Floris Books
Alan Dapré and Yuliya Somina have asserted their rights
under the Copyright, Designs and Patent Act 1988 to
be identified as the Author and Illustrator of this work

The publisher acknowledges subsidy from
Creative Scotland towards the publication
of this volume

MIX
Paper from
responsible sources
FSC
www.fsc.org
FSC® C117931

 Also available as an eBook

British Library CIP data available
ISBN 978-178250-357-6
Printed & bound by MBM Print SCS Ltd, Glasgow

Porridge the Tartan Cat
and the Kittycat Kidnap

Written by Alan Dapré

Illustrated by Yuliya Somina

Young Kelpies

THIS BRAW BOOK BELONGS TO

Porridge the Tartan Cat

Tickle my tum
and you can read it too.

You can even put your
name here, for now:

_____

_____

1
It's only me!

Hi, I'm Porridge the Tartan Cat.

Once upon a tin, I accidentally fell in some tartan paint!

Me-splosh!

Now I'm totally

which is a real word I've just invented.

I live in Tattiebogle Town with the fantastic McFun family. Gadget Grandad, Groovy Gran, Mini Mum, Dino Dad, Roaring Ross and Invisible Isla are always getting into trouble. And I'm *always* getting them out of it.

Me-wow!

Every evening, I curl up and cat-a-log our brawsome adventures. So why not snuggle up beside me and read *Porridge The Tartan Cat and the Kittycat Kidnap*?

It's packed full of amazing shortbread and jokes and words and **ME!**

2

The Bit Where
The Story Starts

One afternoon, Isla and Ross were busy in the kitchen, brushing their favourite cat.

ME!

Mum was baking. Being a famous scientist, she experimented all the time – especially in the kitchen. She loved to create crazy recipes with anything she found in the cupboards. And I mean <u>anything</u>.

So the soups tasted of soap and the spaghetti tasted of shoelaces and the fishy biscuits tasted of fizzy bicarbonate of soda!

Me-yuck!

Mum put on her safety goggles and took a tray of hot super-short shortbread out of the oven. It smoked and smouldered like a crashed meteorite.

"Anyone want to munch my super-short shortbread?" she said, chiselling it into chunks. Two pieces pinged towards the twins, who hurriedly stuffed them in their pockets, 'for later'…

"There's plenty more," trilled Mum. Just then, Dad walked in with a magnifying glass (he loves dinosaurs). He pointed to a muddy trail ahead of him. "These paw prints were made by a rare Porridginus Tartanus Catus!"

 **Me-oops**

Mum pointed to a muddy trail just behind Dad. "And these boot prints were made by Dino Dadus!"

After he had wiped the floor clean with Gadget Grandad's Mop-o-Matic machine, Mum offered him a charred chunk of super-short shortbread.

Dad grabbed two bags of tools. "Sorry, my hands are full. I'm off on a fossil hunt! Bye!" And he dashed out the door.

That left me.

I wasn't hungry. I remembered the last time Mum did a nutty experiment in the kitchen. She tried to make fishy biscuits, but used *almonds* instead of *salmon* because they're almost spelt the same!

 **Me-yuck!**

Mum dropped a lump of shortbread in my favourite bowl and it broke in half. (The bowl,

not the shortbread.) I took a pretend bite and pushed
the shortbread under my cushion, then pulled a
that-was-delicious face.

"I'll get you another... bowl," said Mum.
I thought she was going to say "chunk".

Me-phew

3

A Super-Short Chapter (that is Actually Quite Long)

Even though no one else was keen to try it, Mum couldn't resist a wee taste of her precious super-short shortbread. The sugar on top glittered like shiny diamonds on a lumpy layer of coal.

My fur sprang up and my whiskers tingled. There was magic and danger in the air... and the smell of burnt baking.

Mum took a bite.

"It tastes a bit buttery," she said, a bit spluttery. "And I'm getting a strange squish-squashy sensation inside."

Mum opened her mouth and let out a

BURP!

"Pardon me," she giggled.

And that was when *it happened.*

Mum shrank.

SWOOSH!

Not a lot. Just a little. About as much as a balloon shrinks when you let out some air.

Me-wow!

"That was incredible," gasped Isla.

"That was delicious," Mum squeaked. She took another big bite, and let out another

BURP!

"Pardon me."

Och – it was happening again.

SWOOSH!

Mum wobbled and gasped as the tiled floor rushed towards her. "Now I detect an itchy-titchy feeling... from my itchy nose to my titchy toes."

"Mum! Stop!" cried Ross.

By now, Mum couldn't reach the table. She stood in its shadow and scoffed the crumbs in her hand.

BURP! SWOOSH!

"Pardon me."

Down she went. Smaller and smaller and smaller and smaller until she wasn't any taller than a mouse.

Mmmm. Mouse.

Ross and Isla could not believe their eyes.
They gawped at the tiny person by their feet.

"She's not a grown-up any more," said Isla.

"She's a grown-down," said Ross, trying not to
move his toes in case he trod on her.

Mum had become Mini Mum! She stared up and
up and up and up at the twins and squeaked, "You kids are
terribly tall!"

"You're terribly small," grumbled Isla, kneeling
down on the kitchen floor for a better look. "Food
is meant to make people grow bigger, not smaller.
Somehow super-short shortbread makes you
SUPER-SHORT!"

"If you have any more you'll disappear," said Ross.

"Don't be hasty. It's very tasty," squeaked Mini Mum.

Before you could say 'DON'T CLIMB A CHAIR LEG!' she was climbing a chair leg to reach another chunk.

Seeing the danger, I jumped on the tabletop and batted the tray of super-short shortbread through the open window. It bounced on the grass and scattered crumbly chunks beside six big feathered craws.

Mmmm. Craws.

Half a dozen busy beaks pecked until all the pieces were gone.

Suddenly, a big craw went

BURP!

and shrank as small as a wee bird that hums instead of sings because it doesn't know the words yet.

Mmmm. Humming bird.

BURP!

One by one, the birds burped and shrank. Just like that. Until every craw in the garden could fit in your hand.

Or my food bowl.

Me-yum!

4

The Van

Birds do funny things to a cat.

When I saw the craws I just had to play a game of **CAT**ch. I couldn't stop myself! I forgot all about Mini Mum's super-short problem and flew out the window.

🐾 Me-whoosh! 🐾

Och, it was quicker than boringly pawing the kitchen door. (I *still* don't have a cat flap.)

Pesky wee craws are hard to catch. Catching fishy
biscuits is much easier. I just dip my paw in the box.
I love them so much I could eat them until they came
out of my ears. Then eat them again until they came
out of my ears. Then eat them again until...

🐾 Me-yum! 🐾

That's why I was delighted to see a VAN FULL OF

❤❤ FISHY BISCUITS ❤❤

stop in our street. The van purred like a contented kittycat. I purred like one two because the fishy biscuits were three. I mean, I purred like one too because the fishy biscuits were free. It said so on the side of the van:

**Free Fishy Biscuits –
for Tartan Cats Only!**

🐾 Me-wow! 🐾

ALL those tasty treats were just meant for *me* because I'm the only tartan cat in the whole wide Porridgyverse! I had to get to the van before it drove off. Some cats would get in a flap, but not me. (BECAUSE – AHEM – I STILL DON'T HAVE A CAT FLAP... even after all these books!)

I **CAT**-a-pulted towards the van.

Me-Tw-a-n-g!

By the time I got to the end of this sentence, I was at the garden gate.

"Afternoon, Porridge," puffed our neighbour, Mavis Muckle. "I'm taking Basil out for a stroll."

Actually, Basil the elephant was taking Mavis for a roll.

This was no time for a cat to chat. The van door was swinging in the wind, and waving HELLO at me! Or was it GOODBYE? I ran faster, desperate to taste the delicious treats inside.

 **Me-yum!**

I dived into the van. Deep, deep, deep into a heap, heap, heap of fishy biscuits and **me-yummed** them down like there was no tomorrow. Or the day after.

Or the day after that, or the day after that, or the day after that or the day after that, which is a Tuesday.

I was too busy munching to notice the van door slam shut, or spot the spellling mistake in this sentence.

 Me-oops

The van thundered down the street, faster than a speeding elephant. So fast, the illustrator didn't have time to draw it – sorry! So she drew this picture of a slow-moving snail instead:

5

Little Birdies

The craws and I have a deal: *you scratch my back and I won't scratch yours.* In other words, I promise not to gobble them up, as long as they watch Isla and Ross like hawks when I'm away.

Mmmm. Hawks.

If I miss anything interesting, a little birdie soon tells me what's been going on. The wee craws love

juicy gossip just as much as they love juicy worms.
They sat on a telephone wire and tweeted lots on-line
about the van zooming off.

Ross and Isla spun round at the loud engine sound. They just got a glimpse of the vanishing van, with a tartan scarf billowing out of the back.

"I hope that din didn't scare Porridge," said Ross, looking around for his favourite tartan cat. (ME again!)

Isla glanced at my wee birdie pals on the window ledge. "He's probably outside creeping up on those craws."

"Aye, it is dinner time," said Ross.

Och, forget craws – I'd rather have these fishy biscuits.

 **Me-yum!**

6

The Sack

Night fell suddenly, then picked itself up and whistled a bit and pretended nothing had happened.

Just as suddenly, the van braked hard. The fishy biscuits flew in the air and rained down on me like delicious weather.

CHOMP

CHOMP

CHOMP

30

Before long, the van was empty and I was full.

Me-yum!

I curled up in a corner and closed my eyes, ready for a wee catnap.

My *mega-super-well-OK-not-bad* ears twitched as I heard the driver's door open.

Clunk.

Then I heard the

CLOMP CLOMP CLOMP

of menacing boots.

Then I heard the

SWISH SWISH SWISH

of evil shoelaces.

Then I heard the

CREEK EEK EEK

of the van's back door opening.

Then I heard something **MUCH MUCH MUCH ✗ 107** worse! It brought fear to my heart and a paw to my nose.

TRUMP-PA-RUMP!

Think of the worst smell you know. Double it. Then times it by a big number and sixty-four. Then add a mouldy cabbage, ten stinky dustbins, six skunks and your teacher's smelly socks.

Plus any more revoltingly revolting stuff you can think of. Write it here:

I wanted to flee from the foul smell but a hunched-up figure blocked my way. It had bunched-up fingers and scrunched-up hair that glowed in the moonlight like tangled jellyfish tentacles.

 **Me-shiver!**

My whiskers tingled. My legs shook. My fur stood on end. And my tail fainted. I had no words to describe how scared I felt. So if you think of any, please scribble some in this box.

"Here, kitty-kitty-kittycat," oozed a voice, as warm and soft as molten lava.

I recognised it instantly! For it belonged to a minor character in one of the other *Porridge the Tartan Cat* books. It was...

the pet shop owner!

"Who is she? Tell us more," I hear you whisper, because it's probably late at night and you're meant to be asleep, but you like this book so much you can't put it down, so you're reading it under the covers and turning the pages very quietly.

Before I could tell you more, Windy Wendy whipped out an old laundry sack that had never been washed.

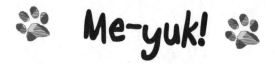

Me-yuk!

Or emptied.

Me-yuk-yuk!

Down came the sack and all went black. All I remember is thinking to myself:

Help!

And then

Help! There are pants on my head!

7

A Wee Problem

🐾 Me-help! 🐾

If only Ross and Isla could rescue me from this stinky sack.

A wee birdie told me later they were too busy trying to re-grow Mini Mum back to normal size.

The twins tried feeding her up.

"This is delicious," squeaked Mini Mum, happily nibbling on a breadcrumb and slurping down a spoonful of soup.

Och, that didn't work.

"Can't you just reverse the super-short shortbread recipe?" asked Ross.

"I would if I knew how I did it in the first place!" squeaked Mini Mum.

Isla gestured at a tall sunflower in the garden. "Maybe we should plant you?"

"Och, no," Mini Mum grumbled. "My clothes would get muddy."

Ross pointed to the oven. "Maybe we should pop you inside until you rise like a cake?"

"I'd be cooked to a crisp!" Mini Mum wailed in a loud whisper.

"Balloons get bigger when you fill them with air!" said Isla, rummaging in a kitchen drawer. She pulled out a plastic pump and grinned at Mini Mum. "All we need to do is blow you up!"

"Och no," squealed Mini Mum in tiny writing. "When things blow up they go BANG!"

The twins sighed. "We'll never solve our wee problem at this rate."

"What wee problem?" asked Mini Mum.

"YOU!"

8

The Pesky Pet Shop

Goats get **KID**napped. I got **CAT**napped.

 Me-sigh!

If only I'd left that nasty fishy van, and those tasty fishy biscuits, alone.

Windy Wendy swung the sack from side to side as she clomped along an echoing passageway. All the swaying and stinky clothes were making me sack-sick.

I was glad to hear a key turn and a door creak open.

The moment Windy Wendy switched on the light, I knew I'd entered her pet shop. The place erupted louder than a noisy volcano. All around me, caged creatures squawked and barked and croaked and whistled and chirped and oinked so crazily I couldn't hear myself blink.

"Haud yer wheesht!" bellowed Windy Wendy, "I cannae hear myself think."

Or stink. The stunned animals fell silent. And a clumsy parrot fell off its perch.

Windy Wendy opened the sack and gawped inside.

I gawped back up at her.

Me-gawp!

They say people look like their pets. Och, Windy Wendy looked like all the pets in the shop mixed together. She had pointy ears, a furry top lip, fingernails like claws and straggly hair. Her nose was round like a rabbit's tail and her boots clomped about like heavy horse hooves.

"I did it," she cackled, with a STINKY look. "Eureka!"

You reeker! I spluttered, remembering that STINKY smell from long ago!

 **Me-gasp!**

That STINKY smell – and STINKY look – suddenly brought back a STINKY old memory. This pongy pet shop was my first home! It was here, just over there, that I had fallen into a tin of tartan paint, all those cat-years ago.

Me-splosh!

Och, *that* was the moment an ordinary kitten became an extraordinary tartan cat!

Suddenly Windy Wendy was all smiles again. Anyone who came in and met her now would have thought she was terribly sweet. After all, she spoke in a terribly sweet way. As sweet as cough syrup. But too much cough syrup is very bad for you. Just like too much Windy Wendy is very bad for you.

And me.

Me-shudder!

This pet shop was a terrible place, full of terribly terrible smells and terribly terrible *terrible* memories.

"I knew I'd trap you in my fishy old van one day," Windy Wendy cackled. "You could never resist a smelly fishy biscuit."

Or ten.

Windy Wendy went on, "Your owners don't love you like I do: I've loved you ever since you fell in that tin of tartan paint." She let the cat out of the bag and put me on the floor. "You splattered tartan paint all over my grotty boots." She beamed at the thought. "You made them look absolutely fabulous! From that moment, I fell in love with

Tartan curtains, tartan carpets, tartan hats, tartan

handbags, tartan lipstick, tartan soup, tartan flowers, tartan ANYTHING!"

Windy Wendy pulled a sad face.

"Most of all, I love YOU, *my* pretty tartan kitty-kitty-kittycat. I was soooooo broken-hearted when naughty Moggiarty chased you away."

MOGGIARTY!!!!!!!!!!

I suddenly remembered him too.

Moggiarty is a cat you never *ever* want to meet, ever. Not in a dark alley or a pet shop. Or this book. It's bad enough seeing a drawing of him.

That monstrous moggy used to chase me all over the shop – all over the shop!

Me-shudder!

I cast a troubled glance at his old cage in the corner. It was empty. Maybe he had been sold while I was away? Or given away as a free gift with a bag of dug biscuits?

Claws crossed.

9

THE ~~WENDY~~ PORIDJ HOUSE

It was late and way past your bedtime.

And mine. But wild-haired Windy Wendy

was still fizzing with energy. She danced in front

of a gloomy mirror at the back of the shop, beside

herself with excitement (get it?), then she turned and

beckoned me with a crooked finger.

"Here, kitty-kitty-kittycat!"

I'm a big tartan cat, not a wee kitty-kitty-kittycat.

I crossed my front paws and stayed put.

She tried again and waggled a fishy biscuit between her fingers.

I'm a big tartan cat, not a wee kitty-kitty-kittycat. I crossed my back paws and stayed put.

Next, Windy Wendy waggled a whole box of fishy biscuits.

I'm a big tartan cat, and I haven't eaten since Chapter 6. I crossed the room and gobbled the lot.

Me-yum!

"I want to show you something," she crooned, in a cough-syrupy voice. Windy Wendy pulled aside a dusty drape to reveal a wooden playhouse. Two words were chalked in dusty letters above the door.

WENDY HOUSE

"Every wee lass called Wendy in the world has a Wendy House," she went on. "And this wee one was mine."

It *was* wee. Windy Wendy was never going to fit into it now, unless she used it as a hat. She clomped to the door and slid open a rusty bolt on the door. The bolt squeaked, the door creaked and I sneaked a peek inside the wee Wendy House.

🐾 Me-wow! 🐾

It carpeted the carpet. It covered the cushion cover. It even enveloped an envelope. Everything inside was TOTALLY

TARTAN!

...except for a totally untartan cat called:

MOGGIARTY!

I was just a wee kitten when I last saw him, but Moggiarty hadn't changed at all. His green eyes were still as hard and shiny as raw sprouts. His fur was still grey as a grubby old snowball. And even though Moggiarty wasn't a real snowball, he always melted whenever Windy Wendy was around.

He loved her more than mice.

Mmmm. Mice.

Moggiarty slinked over to Windy Wendy and greeted her with a loud purr. While he rubbed happily against her boots, she plucked a brass bell from his collar.

"I'm sorry, Moggiarty," she whispered, not sorry at all. "There's only room in ma heart – and the Wendy House – for one cat." Windy Wendy wiped away a crocodile tear, then lifted a trapdoor and put the crocodile back in the cellar. And suddenly let out a terrible

so terribly terrifying that Moggiarty leaped backwards...

...and landed in an empty cage.

Windy Wendy calmly latched the lid.

No longer top dug, er, cat, Moggiarty hissed like a leaky balloon.

SSSSSSSSSSSS

He pawed at the bars, but Windy Wendy only had eyes for me.

MWAH!

And kisses.

Me-yuk!

"You're such a pretty kitty, Porridge." Windy Wendy plonked me onto the tartan cushion where Moggiarty had been sitting only a few paragraphs ago. "I want to keep you forever. From now on, my Wendy House will be your home!"

She scratched out the word WENDY and scrawled PORIDJ instead.

(Everything about Windy Wendy was terrible. Even her spelling.)

 **Me-sigh**

"I've got you a new collar," she trilled, tossing my old one to the floor. "Isn't it gorgeous?"

I felt her fingers clip a thick, metal band around my neck. As soon as she did so, the collar glowed green.

"By the way, I keep the crocodiles in the cellar, just below your cat basket. If you leave this cushion, or mutter the slightest meow, the collar will flash red. The floor will flip down and..."

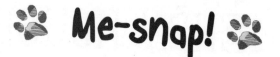

Me-snap!

Smiling now, she hung Moggiarty's old bell on my new collar. "An itty-bitty-kitty-kitty-kittycat like you needs feeding up. Just ring the bell when you want fishy biscuits. Day or night."

And with that, she bolted the door and clomped away.

Never. I thought to myself.

NEVER.

NEVER would I give in and ring the brass bell and eat her delicious nutritious fishy biscuits...

I batted the bell softly.

Ting.

10

No Porridge For Breakfast

Dawn dawned.

The wee craws yawned. They were up bright and early to sing a few notes. And scribble a few notes for me. They crowded (crawded?) around the kitchen window, and saw the twins making Mini Mum's breakfast: a drop of milk on a cornflake.

"Sorry, Mini Mum. We were up half the night but we still can't think how to change you back," yawned Ross.

(That's the trouble with yawning. When somebody or somebirdy starts to yawn, everyone else has to join in.)

"Maybe Porridge can help?" yawned Isla. "He usually saves the day."

"He hasn't touched his fishy biscuits," yawned Mini Mum. "That's not like Porridge. I wonder where he is."

"We haven't seen him since yesterday," said Ross. "Just before that fishy-looking van vanished down the street, trailing a tartan scarf."

"Very *fishy* looking!" agreed Isla. "It was covered in big pictures of fishy biscuits. What if Porridge got stuck inside?"

"Maybe that wasn't a tartan scarf?" Mini Mum gasped. "Maybe it was a tartan tail!"

"Perhaps Porridge has been kidnapped!" cried Ross.

CATnapped. It's **CAT**napped!

Everyone fell silent. They were sure the tail –
er, tale – was true.

"It'll be terrible if he's been taken," cried Ross.
"More terrible than the time he accidentally
swallowed a Christmas tree decoration and got
rushed to the vet with tinsel-itis."

"The best way to find Porridge is to find that van!"
said Isla.

"But what about making Mini Mum bigger?"
added Ross.

"Och, finding Porridge is far more important," she squeaked.

Quite right.

And before you could say let's get some paper
and pens and make some posters... they got some
pens and paper and made some posters.

Which looked exactly, very much, just like this:

MISSING TARTAN CAT!

ANSWERS TO THE NAME PORRIDGE

(IF HE CAN BE BOTHERED)

LAST SEEN IN THIS VAN

IF YOU HAVE ANY INFORMATION,
PLEASE CONTACT ROSS AND ISLA McFUN
AT NUMBER 17 TATTIEBOGLE STREET

When they were finished, it was time to put them up all over Tattiebogle Town.

"Let's do it," said Isla.

So they did.

 Me-missing!

11

Vijay's Café

Mini Mum and the twins flew around town all morning. They were not the only ones. The craws flew around town too. Swooping and circling and doing proper show-off flying as only a bird can do.

"I'm running out of posters," said Isla.

"I'm running out of puff," gasped Mini Mum. "Let's stop and have lunch."

"Good idea," said Ross.

"Vijay's Café is only a hop, step and jump away," squeaked

Mini Mum, hitching a ride on a passing frog. They hopped off the pavement onto a step, then jumped through an open door.

"Didn't you go to school with Vijay?" asked Ross, scooping Mum up and placing her on a table inside.

"Aye, when I was wee."

"You still are wee," giggled Isla. "Over lunch, we can chat about how to make you bigger. I'm hungry."

Vijay got his skates on and came over very quickly. His four-wheeled footwear helped him serve customers in super-quick time.

WHEEEEEEEEEE–SQUEEEK–WHEEEEEEEEEE–EEK

"Hello, Vijay," squeaked Mini Mum, waving at him from an upturned cup.

"Hi pal. You look different." He peered down. "Your hair is shorter."

"So is the rest of me," said Mini Mum.

"It's a long story," said Isla.

"Short story." Ross grinned. "Mini Mum became super-short when she ate some super-short shortbread!"

"I'm still a wee bit hungry," she squeaked, opening the menu.

Isla took a big breath and smelled... nothing.

Not a sausage. And if you put this book to your nose and *really* sniff you won't smell a sausage either.

Probably because this is just a book. An ordinary book about an extraordinary cat.

Everything on the menu was crossed out, apart from the hot cross buns, which were already crossed.

"All my fresh food has been eaten by beasties from the pet shop next door," sighed Vijay. "I keep this place spotless – even the spotty tablecloths – but last week a customer found a mouse in her moussaka and another had a rat in his ratatouille. It was terrible!"

"You mean Windy Wendy's pet shop?" asked Ross.

"Aye, the pongy one. They must be escaping from the smell." Vijay lowered his voice. "Never go in unless you have a cold. Or a clothes peg. Or an excuse never to go in."

"We were going to put up a poster there after lunch." Isla showed Vijay the picture she had drawn. "We think our tartan cat vanished in *this* van."

"It looks a bit small," joked Vijay. "How did Porridge fit in?"

"Och, this is just a wee drawing," giggled Isla. "The real van is much bigger."

Vijay took the twins and Mini Mum to look out of a window at the back of the café. "Is it as big as that van over there?"

"Yes!" whooped Isla, "because that *is* the van we're looking for! Who owns it?"

Vijay explained. "My neighbour, Windy Wendy. She drives the van at night, and parks behind her pet shop every morning. She has an odd offer on: free fishy biscuits to tartan cats only."

Isla shivered. "That does sound fishy."

"I hope Porridge is OK," said Ross.

Quick, let's go to the next chapter and check if I am!

12

Something Fishy

If you look closely at the picture below you will see a stuffed tartan cushion. If you look *very* closely you will see a stuffed tartan cat on a stuffed tartan cushion.

 Me-burp!

I *had* planned to scoff fishy biscuits until I built up enough strength to snap my shiny collar and bash my way to freedom. But now I was so stuffed I couldn't move. I couldn't speak either, in case I set off my collar alarm and woke the crocs.

 Me-snap!

Moggiarty rattled his cage and growled, "Your noisy bell kept me awake last night."

My unhappy tum grumbled back.

G-RRRR-UUMMMMBBLE!

"You're only grumbling because those fishy biscuits were stale," snickered Moggiarty. "They're rotten old rejects from the Fishy Biscuit Factory! You should never have come back here. Go home. You're about as welcome as a sprout on a chocolate birthday cake."

Home.

It seemed like only yesterday that I was there. (Um, probably because it *was* yesterday.)

Home.

The marvellous McFun family only feed me *fresh* fishy biscuits. So fresh, they practically swim into my food bowl!

🐾 Me-sigh 🐾

I missed them more than clumsy cats miss mice.

Mmmm. Mice.

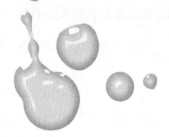

13

Falling Out

Windy Wendy spent all morning feeding the animals. She was feeding the grasshoppers to the lizards and the lizards to the buzzards when something unexpected happened. The pet shop door creaked open and the twins walked in!

Me-phew!

I wasn't expecting that! I squinted through a crack in the boarded-up window of the ~~WENDY~~ PORIDJ HOUSE.

🐾 **Me-yay!** 🐾

My *mega-super-well-OK-not-bad* eyes spied Mini Mum in Isla's hood. Then my *mega-super-well-OK-not-bad* ears heard her whisper to the twins.

"Keep a look out for trouble. And Porridge."

"It's the same thing," muttered Isla.

Charming.

Hidden in the gloom at the back of the room, all I could do was look on in silence. I couldn't meow or move off my cushion without setting off the pesky alarm.

Windy Wendy kept her gaze on the trembling twins. Her smile was wide but her eyes were narrow, and full of nasty suspicion. And nasty gritty stuff in the corners.

"How can I help you?" warbled Windy Wendy.

"We've lost our cat. Have you seen a tartan cat around?"

"No."

"What about this van?" asked Ross. He handed her a poster.

Windy Wendy barely glanced at the picture. She paced about with a shifty look on her face and wiped away a trickle of sweat with a handy hamster.

"NO!" she said, raising her voice.

"Really?" said Ross. He ran to the back of the shop and raised the window blind. Outside, the fishy van was clearly visible, parked in the passage behind the pet shop.

"I've never seen that van before!" fibbed Windy Wendy. She yanked down the blind with astonishing speed.

SLATTER-CLATTER!

As the last of the daylight left the room, Mini Mum glimpsed three words scrawled above a wee wooden door:

PORIDJ ~~WENDY~~ HOUSE

Mini Mum jumped in surprise and toppled from Isla's hood. I blinked in astonishment as she fell between the bars of Moggiarty's cage! Now she was in terrible danger – I had to warn the twins!

But how?

"Out!" snapped Windy Wendy. "My pet shop is shut!"

"Let's go," sighed Ross.

I forgot all about the cranky crocs and tried to yowl as loud as I could, but my throat was too dry from munching those stale fishy biscuits.

"Don't come back," cried Windy Wendy, locking the door behind the twins.

Och, they still didn't know Mini Mum had fallen out of Isla's hood! She was in big trouble. She had tumbled into a bed of straw that belonged to the meanest, moodiest cat in town: **MOGGIARTY!**

14
Hide and Squeak

Windy Wendy settled down for a snooze while Mini Mum, trapped in Moggiarty's cage, squeaked like a mouse.

"Somebody help me!"

🐾 Me-shhh! 🐾

Never squeak like a mouse when a cat is about.

Moggiarty stared suspiciously at the straw then fished around with a curious paw. How scary is that? Och, at least a ghostillion, which is a scarily big number I just made up.

Got you! he hissed, plucking her out like a lucky dip prize.

SPLINK!

I could hardly look. I was afraid of what Moggiarty might do to her. Eat her with relish?

"I'll eat her just as she is," said Moggiarty, who didn't like relish very much.

He held up his wee two-legged lunch and licked his lips. Nothing could stop him munching Mini Mum now.

Except that!

Moggiarty leaped like a startled cat because he was startled and a cat. (I've used that joke before but I am recycling. It's a very good thing to do. Ask your teacher.)

He crashed against his rusty bars and sent the cage toppling to the floor.

SPLANG-FLANG-A-DANG!

The dented cage tumbled open and Moggiarty stumbled out. He reached through the bent bars and pawed at the straw.

"Where's she gone now?" the grey cat grunted.

He asked a bored-looking owl, who didn't give a hoot (get it?!).

Mini Mum had vanished.

Will we ever see her again? Will you ever read about her again? You'll find out in a really exciting chapter called The Really Exciting Chapter!

(Cue dramatic music.)

DUN-DUN-DUUUUN!

(And dramatic rustling of pages.)

RUSTLE-RUSTLE-RUUUUSTLE!

15

The Really Exciting Chapter!

I was still on my tartan cushion in the ~~WENDY~~ PORIDJ
HOUSE when a wee friendly face appeared at the
boarded up window.

Mini Mum!

She had climbed up the side of the wee house
on a dusty old spider's web. "I knew you were here," she
whispered. "I saw a sign that said ~~WENDY~~ PORIDJ HOUSE."

Mini Mum was talking quietly, but not quietly
enough. Moggiarty spun round at the sound, ready to

pound the ground like a hound.

"Catch me if you can," squeaked Mini Mum, squeezing between the wooden strips that covered the broken window.

Moggiarty missed her by a whisker! (She was hanging off one of mine.) He slammed against the side of the wee house and slid down instead!

"I'll take a wee rest," puffed Mini Mum. She twanged off my whisker onto the soft tartan cushion. As she did so, a grumpy grey cat rattled the doorknob. A moment later, Moggiarty keeked through the crack in the boarded-up window.

"Let me in, let me in," he growled, with a wolfish grin.

"No, no, not by the hair on my tartan chinny chin chin," I whispered, going all Three Little Pigs on him.

Moggiarty began to huff and puff about how great he was at blowing down houses, but it all was just a lot of hot air. Och, the playhouse was 100% windproof.

It had to be, when Windy Wendy was about.

16

Cat On a Not Tin Roof

For those of you who have picked this book up in a shop or library, and randomly opened it at this page, here is the fabutastic story so far.

I was trapped, with Mini Mum, in

THE WORST PET SHOP IN THE WORLD

and here is a certificate to prove it:

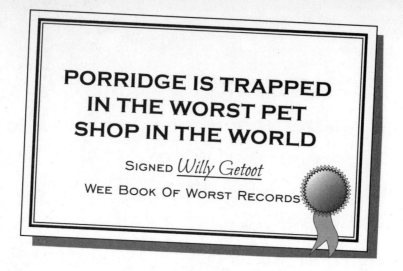

PORRIDGE IS TRAPPED IN THE WORST PET SHOP IN THE WORLD

SIGNED *Willy Getoot*

WEE BOOK OF WORST RECORDS

We were stuck in the ~~WENDY~~ **PORIDJ** HOUSE, over the crocodile trapdoor, with a wolfish cat trying to get in by the hairs on his chinny chin chin.

A beautiful beantiful smell wafted through a low hole in the wall. It tickled my nose...

 **Me-sniff!**

Windy Wendy sniffed too, even though she had fallen asleep with her feet resting on a hibernating tortoise.

"Beaaaannns," she muttered between her snores.

She was completely unaware of the grey cat who had sneaked his way over and was now swinging from a parrot cage above her head.

Mini Mum and I watched in amazement as Moggiarty clung on and swung forward and back. What was he trying to do?

Squawwwk

Wwwindy Wwendy

wwwake up squawwwk

That was Carrot, the orange parrot, by the way. He was talking and squawking loudly inside his swinging cage.

Moggiarty let go, flew towards us and dug his claws deep in the roof of the ~~WENDY~~ PORIDJ HOUSE.

Windy Wendy opened one eye. "Stop that squawking," she shouted, "or I'll crunch an orange Carrot for lunch!" She sniffed and suddenly had a better idea. "I smell beaaannnns, beans, glorious beans! Nothing can beat them. I really MUST eat them!"

❧ Me-wow! ❧

She leapt from her chair and flicked her tongue in the air like a snake (but not an adder because she was rubbish at maths). She slithered past the lizards and bent down by the hole in the wall.

"The smell is coming from Vijay's Café," she muttered.

I had a brawsome thought. *If a mini smell could come in, maybe a Mini Mum could get out?*

"I neeeeed beaaannnns," said Windy Wendy, lumbering to the pet shop door, hungry as a bear. She didn't see Moggiarty clinging to the roof of the ~~WENDY~~ PORIDJ HOUSE. At the door, Windy Wendy reached into a hiding place in her whiffy right boot and plucked out a rusty key.

"See you later, alligator. And badger and cockroach and dragonfly and emu and flea..." she cackled alphabetically, flying out of the shop like a witch on an invisible broomstick.

Ker-likkk!

The key turned. I was locked in! All alone, apart from Mini Mum, Moggiarty and 722 other animals, not counting the ants, because that would take ages.

17

Saved By The Bell

With Windy Wendy out of the way, Moggiarty was free to do as he pleased. He dangled off the roof of the ~~WENDY~~ **PORIDJ** HOUSE and batted the bolt on the door.

Bat　　　　Bat　　　　Bat

Three bats flew over his head.

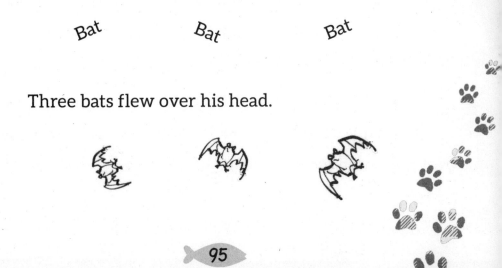

"I don't like the sound of that," squeaked Mini Mum, terror flashing across her tiny face.

I swiftly hid her in my thick furry coat. Just in time. The door bolt slid open, and so did the door. A grinning grey cat dropped to the floor. I shrank back on my cushion, unable to move in case the cranky crocs got me.

 Me-snap!

"Where is that tasty two-legged treat?" the grey cat hissed, licking its paw and looking for Mini Mum.

"I ate it," I fibbed. I poked out my tongue and showed him Mini Mum's tiny goggles.

"That was greedy!" growled Moggiarty, prowling around my tartan cushion. By now, he wasn't looking at me – his eyes were fixed on his old brass bell.

"You're in deep trouble after I get that back."

He swiped at the bell with a pesky paw.

TING TING TING TING!

"You're in deep trouble now," I whispered.

"Why?" he hissed.

"You're not on the cushion."

A flap flew open above Moggiarty's head and a flood of stale fishy biscuits cascaded onto him. Soon I was staring at a big biscuity mountain, with only the tip of a tail sticking out.

"I'll get you for this," said a thin voice. Moggiarty had no room to move his paws, only his jaws. There was a muffled munch-a-crunch from deep within, as he slowly tried to chomp his way out.

🐾 Me-yuk! 🐾

I'd rather eat this book.

"Thanks Porridge!" Mini Mum climbed out of my fur and ran to the open door of the pesky ~~WENDY~~ PORIDJ HOUSE. "Let's get out of here!"

She beckoned me over but I shook my head. I gave my collar a sad tug, then jabbed my tail at the floor.

A terrible gnashing and clashing of teeth came from below.

SNAP SNAP SNAP

The crocodiles were playing cards, to see who would crunch a tartan cat for lunch. I swung my front paws open and shut and mimed their big jaws.

SNAP SNAP SNAP

"Crocodiles!" gasped Mini Mum. "If you're on the menu, there's no time to waste. I'll get the twins."

I nodded quickly. It was all I could do!

She paused at the door of the ~~WENDY~~ PORIDJ HOUSE and glanced around the gloomy room. "How can I get out of the pet shop?"

 Me-think!

Och, I knew the answer to that – *through the wee hole where the smell got in!* I jabbed my *mega-super-well-OK-not-bad* tail towards it, and Mini Mum ran off. My *mega-super-well-OK-not-bad* ears heard her faint sniff.

"I've caught a faint whiff of Vijay's beans! I won't be long!"

Skirting from skirting board to skirting board, Mini Mum got to the small hole without being seen by any more hungry animals.

 Me-phew!

One cheery wave later and she was gone. Now I was all alone again, apart from all those animals I listed earlier. All 722.

And the ants.

And dribbly, nibbly Moggiarty under a pile of fishy biscuits. And a murderous crowd of crocodiles.

 Me-gulp!

18

Fang Bungler

My *mega-super-well-OK-not-bad* ears heard the twins' anxious footsteps, pacing this way and that by the van at the back of the pet shop.

"That Windy Wendy is hiding something," said Ross.

"Aye, it's time we checked out this fishy-looking van," said Isla. "Maybe Porridge is stuck inside?"

The twins took a quick look, full of hope.

It was full of empty. I'd eaten all the fishy biscuits inside, remember?

"It's quiet without Porridge..." said Ross sadly.

"Mini Mum's quiet too... I haven't heard a squeak from her since we visited the pet shop," said Isla. "I think she's fallen asleep."

"Or fallen out!" gasped Ross.

The twins checked Isla's hood – it was empty!

"Quick, back to the pet shop!" Isla cried.

But the door was locked, and when the worried twins banged on it, there was no answer.

"What should we do?" asked Ross. "Maybe Vijay has seen her?"

The twins trudged back to the café. I heard their sad sighs and I let out a quiet sob. I was sad. They were sad. Even the crocodiles in the cellar below me were sad, but that only made them **SNAPPIER**.

"Cheer up," said Vijay when he saw their glum faces. "You'll find Porridge... just like I found these beans hidden at the back of a cupboard."

He showed them a big pan of bubbling beans.

Mmmm. Beans.

"It's not just Porridge, we've lost Mini Mum now too!" sighed Ross.

"Have you seen her?" asked Isla.

"No," said Vijay. "Did you lose her in the pet shop?"

Ross shrugged. "Windy Wendy locked it up. We can't get in."

"That's because she's here," whispered Vijay. "She can't get enough of my brawsome beans."

The kids turned to see Windy Wendy sitting in the far corner, eating a bucket of beans. She had her sad face on, which was just like her happy face. And her grumpy face. And her I-can-juggle-frogs face...

HAPPY   SAD   GRUMPY   I CAN
JUGGLE FROGS

Vijay dropped his voice and his dishcloth: "If she's lost in the pet shop, Mini Mum is in *maximum* danger. She might be chomped by a chameleon or flattened by a flatfish! Or worse – if Windy Wendy finds out she's been trespassing in the shop!"

"We need a way to get back inside," said Ross.

Just then, Windy Wendy waltzed around the

tables towards the counter. "I'm the best waltzer in town," she boasted. (Even though the one at the funfair was way better.)

"Can I help you?" asked Vijay.

"Bring me another bucket of beans!" she boomed, before turning to the twins with her sad face on. "What a pity you weans lost your tartan cat."

"We'll find him," said Ross firmly.

Windy Wendy shrugged. She fished in her pocket and pulled out a wee bug. "Why not take home Buggy the poisonous fang bungler instead?"

"That's a squeaky dung beetle," said Isla, who was wise in the ways of smelly six-legged insects.

"Buggy just needs oiling," fibbed Windy Wendy. "But beware! One bite and you will turn into a clumsy zombie."

Vijay skated over to Windy Wendy and said, "Please take these beans – and that bug – away. I don't want any more beasties in my café."

He handed her a huge bucket, and threw open the door.

Windy Wendy glared at the twins. "After ma lunch, I always have a wee nap. So the pet shop is shut until I wake up. No customers allowed – or I'll create a big stink!"

On her way out, Windy Wendy accidentally-on-purpose chucked Buggy on the floor.

"Oopsie," she giggled, waltzing off down the street... She still wasn't the best waltzer in town.

Wasting no time, Buggy scuttled into a hole in the wall. Wasting no thyme, Vijay skated over and plugged the hole with a clump of parsley.

19

Someone Should Write a Book About This

"She'll gobble those beans in a flash," said Vijay, pleased with himself. "Beans make people sleepy. It won't be long before we hear her snoring. I put in EXTRA beans to make her EXTRA sleepy."

Ross and Isla smiled at each other. This was their chance to find Mini Mum *and* look for more Porridgy clues.

Me-phew

Just then, the twins heard squeaking from the hole in the wall. The squeaks grew louder.

"Sounds like Buggy the poisonous fang bungler is back!" whispered Ross.

The three of them crept towards the parsley-packed hole to listen.

SCUTTLE SCUTTLE SCUTTLE SCUTTLE

SQUEAK SQUEAK SQUEAK

...and got a huge shock when the six-legged mini-beast burst out with Mini Mum on his back! She was riding him as if he was a six-legged pony called Sparkle or Misty (not Buggy because that sounds like a pram).

"Hi, twins!" she squeaked. Her wee trusty steed reared on two legs and neighed like a mouse.

Mmmm. Mouse.

"Well, blow me down with a wonky helicopter." Vijay fell back in amazement and a chair. "It's Mini Mum!"

Everyone patted her head (and then washed their hands because she had been riding a really smelly dung beetle).

"Where did you go?" asked Isla.

"I saw a big sign on a wee ~~WENDY~~, I mean, PORIDJ HOUSE," she answered. "It was such a shock I fell out of your hood."

"Did you find Porridge?" asked Ross.

"Yes, but he's still trapped inside, guarded by crocodiles! I think Windy Wendy wants to keep him forever!"

"Never!" said the twins together.

"Forever!" repeated Mini Mum. "And it gets worse – there's another cat in there and he's dangerous."

"We have to save him quick," said Ross. "But how?"

"We work as a wee team." Isla pulled a piece of super-short shortbread from her pocket.

"You'll be in big trouble if you eat that!" squeaked Mini Mum.

"It's very dangerous being wee. You might get chewed by a Chihuahua or squished by a squid!"

"Too late," said the twins, each taking a nibble of the rather incredible... and rather inedible... super-short shortbread.

The twins let out a wee **BURP!** and **SWOOSH!** grew down instead of up.

Within a minute they were minute.

Vijay knelt down carefully and said, "While you're gone, I'll look in my old recipe books. I'll cook up something special to get you three big again."

"This way, twins," said Mini Mum. Her gallant steed rose on two legs and galloped bravely into the hole in the wall. The twins ran after her, their tiny footsteps echoing. Echoing. Echoing. Echoing.

"Someone should write a book about this," said Vijay, shaking his head in wonder...

20

Not A Pretty Sight

Windy Wendy plonked herself in her favourite chair, hungry as a dustbin lorry.

She tipped up the big bucket of beans and greedily guzzled them all in one go.

SLOPPA-PLOPPA-GLOPP-GLOPP-GLOPPA!

It was not a pretty sight, and I really hope the illustrator does not draw you a picture of it:

Sorry about that.

She ended her meal with a

so **TERRIFYING** that all the hedgehogs inside

the shop went green, rolled into spiky balls and

pretended to be conker cases. The ~~WENDY~~ PORIDJ
HOUSE shuddered and its door slammed shut, jarring
the bolt back into place.

I was trapped inside with Moggiarty!

Lucky for me, he was still trapped under a
mountain of fishy biscuits.

"That was luvvalicious," Windy Wendy cackled,
picking her teeth with an unlucky stick insect.
She glanced around the cluttered pet shop and
grumbled. "I need more hippos and wasps and
giraffes and extra hippos."

Carrot the parrot squawked glumly above her head. "And fewer parrots." She rose from her chair and pulled a thick cover over his cage. Then she slumped back wearily and closed her tired eyes.

A moment later she heard a squeak from the back of the room. It came from near the shadowy ~~WENDY~~ PORIDJ HOUSE. Och, the pet shop was always full of annoying animal noises.

"Quiet. It's ma naptime." She sleepily launched a boot into the darkness.

SPLABBA-*BOING!*

It booted a hole through the boarded-up window of the ~~WENDY~~ PORIDJ HOUSE! The boot spun to a stop by the heap of fishy biscuits.

Moggiarty wiggled his tail tip in disgust at the smell. The battered boot ponged like a year-old school dinner.

Me-shudder!

The wee house shuddered too. Windy Wendy was asleep and snoring so loudly that the whole shop rattled. *Especially the rattlesnakes.*

I heard some more squeaking... it was Mini Mum!

"I'm back with reinforcements," she squeaked, climbing through the ~~WENDY~~ PORIDJ HOUSE window with the wee twins by her side.

"We'll soon get you out of here," whispered Ross. "Once we get down."

"We'll have to jump on the cushion," said Isla. "One... two... three... Go!"

They leaped all at once...

BA-BOINGGG!

My three would-be rescuers bounced off the cushion...

...and tumbled inside Windy Wendy's stinky tartan boot.

 Me-pooh!

They staggered out, holding their breath... and a rusty key!

"I banged my head on this," grumbled Ross. "I wonder why it was in Windy Wendy's boot?"

I had definitely seen that key before – in Chapter 16.

She'd plucked it from her boot to lock up the pet shop. I purred with happiness and told the twins we could work together to open the front door.

(Unfortunately they can't speak Cat. So I picked up the key and mimed opening a big door and walking through. Then closing the door and walking home and eating a big bowl of fishy biscuits.)

"A-ha! It must be the key for the shop door," said Isla. "That means it's the key to our escape!"

"How do we reach the keyhole?" groaned Ross, rubbing his head.

"Porridge could do it," said Isla, as she dragged the heavy key onto the cushion.

"He can't leave the Wendy house, or we'll all be eaten by crocodiles!" warned Mini Mum.

I froze at the thought. Then I suddenly thawed and clawed at the collar until hot sparks flew off it.

 **Me-sigh**

It was still good as new.

I slumped on my cushion, a fed-up feline, feeling sorry for myself.

⚬° BURRRP! °⚬

Everyone looked at the cat, still buried in stale fishy biscuits. We noticed his nose was poking out, as green as a poorly gooseberry. He had something to say. "I'll help you escape, if you help me."

I had a wee think about that.

One think later:

NEVER!

"You poor thing," said Isla, walking over and stroking Moggiarty's trapped tail. "This is no place for a handsome cat like you."

The grumpy, grey cat blinked in surprise. *No one* had ever said anything nice to Moggiarty before, probably because he was a grumpy grey cat. Isla tickled his chin and he trembled like an electric toothbrush.

21

Seeing Red

"Please help me, Porridge," pleaded Moggiarty. Isla's kindness in the last chapter must have warmed his cold heart. "I don't want to be in Windy Wendy's pet shop any more. Free me now and we'll give that big bag o wind a lesson she'll never forget."

Me-ok

I dug like a DUG into the big heap of biscuits. (How uncool is that? Never tell anyone. Not even yourself.) By the end of this paragraph Moggiarty was free!

Suddenly his eyes narrowed, and he sprang out through the broken window. Gone like the wind. If the wind was grey and had fur.

"He's going to tell Windy Wendy we're here!" squeaked Mini Mum, diving for cover in my fur. The twins dived in too.

"Porridge, can you escape through the window?" squeaked Ross, clinging on by my ear.

I shook my head. *Ma big bahookie would get stuck.*

 **Me-sigh**

Then, just as suddenly as he had left, Moggiarty was back! He squeezed through the window and dropped onto my cushion.

SNAP SNAP SNAP!

"Nae worries, it's not the crocs," said Moggiarty, seeing my furry frightened face. He held a snapping turtle close to my glowing green collar.

SNAP!

Its powerful jaws bit the collar in two.

Me-phew!

It fell from my neck and dropped onto my cushion... and I was free!

Me-phew!

But wait – the collar bounced again and drop-ped

to a stop on the floor of the wee wooden house. It began to flash red for danger (and if you take away the d you get anger too).

🐾 Me-oops! 🐾

BLANG-A-LANG-A-DANG!

An alarm bell rang and the floor tilted down. One turtle and two cats clung to the cushion, while the Wee Yins clung to me! Then the cushion started sliding like a sledge down the slope.

Slowly...

then faster…

towards the cellar!

I saw restless shapes splashing, yellow eyes flashing and sharp teeth clashing in the dank, dark water below.

Save yourself! Turn the page!

22
Green Again

The flashing red collar was sliding just ahead of us. Soon it would tumble among the crocs. Then we'd be next!

Suddenly I had a brawsome idea.

I curled my tail around the turtle. Then held it out as far as I could in front of us.

Me-strreetccchhhhh!

"Grab the flashing red collar, and make it snappy!"
I said, totally talking Turtle.

(It turtley understood me too!)

SNAP!

The collar was safely clamped in the turtle's jaws.
I hauled him back onto the cushion.

Me-phew!

The collar stopped flashing red and glowed green instead, making the floor tilt up suddenly, away from the crocodiles, who scowled at the thought of missing their lunch. And then they were gone.

See you later, alligator. (Close enough.)

We paused to hear if Windy Wendy had been awoken by the alarm, but she carried on snoring. We all lay panting on the lovely *flat* floor of the ~~WENDY~~ PORIDJ HOUSE.

Me-pant pant pant

"Well done, everyone," squeaked Mini Mum.

Ahem. I was the hero. OK, with a wee bit of help from that turtle.

Now I no longer had the horrid flashing collar locked around my neck, we could finally escape the pesky ~~WENDY~~ PORIDJ HOUSE. I put the rusty key in my mouth and yowled, "Letshh getshh outshh ofshh shhere."

But how?

Moggiarty pointed to the window.

"I'll getshh shtuck," I muttered.

"Just do it," he hissed. "And I'll follow."

A moment later I was stuck! Most of me was out the wee house, but ma big bahookie was still inside!

Told you!

Not for long. Moggiarty picked up the snapping turtle and it BIT MY BAHOOKIE!

SNAP!

Me-OWWWWWwwww!

I flew through the air like a furry football and splat-flat-cat-landed in Windy Wendy's lap.

She woke with a jump. And a terrible

The big blustery blast blew her onto her feet. I flew up ^{up} ^{up} off her lap and clawed the parrot cage! Windy Wendy didn't see me hanging above her head. Instead, she saw Moggiarty, halfway out of the ~~WENDY~~ PORIDJ HOUSE.

 Me-gulp

"I'm fed up with you, Moggiarty!" She strode over, grabbed her boot and snatched the cat. "Soon my piranhas will be fed up with you too."

Moggiarty swung upside-down as she clomped across the pet shop. He saw everything the wrong way up, except for the bats, who were the right way down.

"Oopsie. I forgot to feed these hungry fishes yesterday." Windy Wendy dangled poor Moggiarty over the piranha tank.

She forgot something else too: to look up!

23

Bite Like A Crocodile

There was only one way to save Moggiarty. I let go of the parrot cage...

...and dropped on Windy Wendy, bahookie first. She fell backwards and I squashed her flat like a pressed flower (probably a stinkwort).

"I thought you loved me, Porridge!" she wailed. Her arm stuck out, still clutching a grey cat. With the other arm she flung me away from her.

I said nothing. I still had the pet-shop key in my mouth, remember?

Let me go, hissed Moggiarty, but he was still on the pesky piranha menu.

"Once I've fed Moggiarty to the fish I'll see if they like Porridge too." Windy Wendy staggered to her feet and swaggered back to the piranha tank. She dangled Moggiarty over the side, just inches from a sea of snapping jaws.

I tucked the key into my collar and yowled, *No, you don't!*

I thundered across the room, zinging and springing from cage to cage. When the animals saw me they roared with delight. Windy Wendy gulped hard.

Bite like a crocodile... spring like a flea!

Me-smoosh!

(I bit her bahookie.)

OW-WOW-WOW-WOW-WOWTCH!

Windy Wendy threw her hands in the air – and Moggiarty too!

As he flew overhead, I held up the key. He grabbed it, slotted it skilfully in the door lock, and...

Sklunk-ker-likkk

Moggiarty swung on a heavy handle and dropped to the floor. The shop door creaked open and

BASHED

Windy Wendy's bahookie again!

OW-WOW-WOW-WOW-WOWTCH!

The Wee Yins clambered onto my back and watched in amazement as Windy Wendy tottered and spun into a stack of fat sacks, then skidded sideways and knocked open a trunk of skunks.

All at once, a bad stink filled the air and the skunks blamed it on Windy Wendy, even though it was probably one of them.

Me-pong!

Next, a crate of chickens crashed to the ground and the birds broke free. Soon the pet shop was a flurry of feathers and fur and ants and antlers and whiskers and husks and tusks and bugs and slugs and...

It was time to go. The sunny pavement looked warm and inviting. I darted forward...

"Where do you think you are going?" Windy Wendy blocked the doorway with her bruised bahookie. "Get back in your ~~WENDY~~ PORIDJ HOUSE or I'll squash you flat with this baby hippo."

(She was actually holding a baby walrus, but it wasn't the right time to correct her.)

I felt a wee tug on my right ear.

"Let's get rid of that big old meanie!" said Ross.

"She can't hold us all in!" Isla shouted. "Let's start a stampede!"

We ran around the room opening cages, then, like speedy sheepdugs, we herded the animals towards Windy Wendy and the open door. All the creatures were hungry for food and revenge...

Mmmm. Food.

Windy Wendy squawked in terror and tumbled backwards onto the tortoise, who carried her through the door, really, really, really, really, really slowly. Squawking parrots and parakeets pecked at the petrified pet-shop owner, while the rest of the animals followed the tortoise out into the sunshine.

Me-phew!

"Get back inside!" screeched Windy Wendy.

"What have I ever done tae you?"

Locked us all up, Moggiarty hissed. *But not any more!*

An army of animals chased her down the street.

They were all free as birds now – especially the birds.

"That's the last we'll see of her," whooped Ross, really

quietly because he was still wee.

"Great teamwork," said Mini Mum, giving us a wee hug.

"I love happy endings."

So do I. But this isn't the end yet. We still have to go to the next chapter and hope Vijay can make everyone big again.

See you there.

24

A Recipe For Success

Back at the café, all was calm. Vijay was quietly tidying up after lots of baking. He had re-stocked his kitchen, and it was now cluttered with open cookbooks. There were stacks of sticky stuff in the sink.

"It's a bit of a mess," he mumbled happily to himself, then he clapped with delight when he saw me come in and vanished in a cloud of flour.

"Porridge! You're free at last!" He reappeared with a bright smile that lit up the café. When he saw

Moggiarty, his bright smile lit up the whole street!
"What a gorgeous wee pal you've made too!"

Moggiarty stuck his tail up, jumped onto the counter and padded over to Vijay, leaving a trail of floury footprints. He rubbed his whiskery chin against Vijay's whiskery chin, and purred like a happy motorbike.

So that was that. Moggiarty winked at me, curled up in a cake tin, and made himself at home!

"How did you get on?" asked Ross.

"All my recipes were half-baked at first," said Vijay. "Then I found one that might do the trick. It's ma great-great granny's great-great recipe for self-raising shortbread."

I keeked through the glass oven door.

Me-yum!

"It looks baked to purr-fection," said Moggiarty, stealing my line. Fortunately humans can't speak Cat anyway.

Vijay pulled on his oven gloves and took out a hot tray. The self-raising shortbread smelt delicious.

He put it down and Moggiarty fanned it with his tail.

Cool.

The Wee Yins quickly picked a chunk each. They didn't want to be the size of a mouse any more.

Mmmm. Mouse.

"I hope it works," squeaked Mini Mum.

So did I. We were running out of flour. *And chapters.*

Vijay shrugged. "Super-short shortbread made you all small, so I'm hoping self-raising shortbread will make you all tall!"

He moved a few tables and stacked some chairs, making a space in the middle of the room. Then he scooped up the Wee Yins and placed them gently on the floor. He wished them luck and took a step back.

"Let's take a nibble and see what happens," said Isla.

After nibble number one, they said they felt a pleasant fizzing and a bit of a stretch. With more nibbles the feeling grew and so did they – from both ends like a blown-up party balloon – until they were all as tall as me.

"So far so good," muttered Ross. "This recipe is magic."

Vijay winked. "So was ma great-great granny."

Moggiarty watched, wide-eyed, as his earlier prey stretched like a piece of pulled chewing gum.

Soon the twins were the size of twins.

Purrfect.

Ross and Isla dropped their leftovers into the bin. Meanwhile, Mini Mum crunched the last chunk of her self-raising shortbread. It went straight down and she went straight up until she wasn't mini any more. She was the size of a mum.

 Me-phew!

She stared at the remaining self-raising shortbread in the tin. "Maybe just one more wee piece?"

You're purrfect as you are! I purred, batting the shortbread pieces out of the window. Just to make sure nobody got any more **BIG** ideas.

25

Back Like A Bad Smell

"PORRRRRRRRRRRRRRRRRRRRRR..."

The strangest sound floated in through the window as the last of Vijay's shortbread somersaulted out.

Still yelling loudly, Windy Wendy turned up at the window like a bad Penny, whoever she is. She was climbing in, big crumbly shortbread erupting from her mouth like rocks from a volcano. **"...RRRIDGE IS MINE. GIVE ME THAT TARTAN CAT!"**

She swallowed hard.

 **Me-help!**

"Oh no! She's scoffed the self-raising shortbread," shouted Vijay. "Abandon café!"

-9-

We scarpered down the sunlit street. A huge shadow chased us, growing all the time.

"Look at me!" whooped Windy Wendy. "I'm as big as a bus."

In just two strides she was by my side.

Me-help!

"Got you!" She scooped me up between giant fingers, because she was now officially a giant.

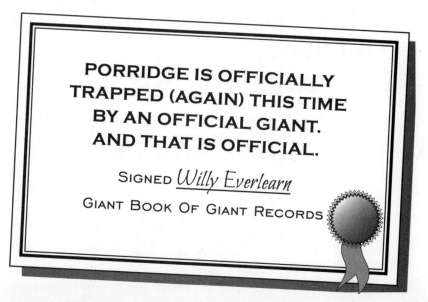

PORRIDGE IS OFFICIALLY TRAPPED (AGAIN) THIS TIME BY AN OFFICIAL GIANT. AND THAT IS OFFICIAL.

SIGNED *Willy Everlearn*

GIANT BOOK OF GIANT RECORDS

Windy Wendy cradled me in her huge hands as if I was the most precious baked bean in the world, even though I'm a tartan cat. She towered above the Big Yins, wobbling and wheezing like a leaky bouncy castle.

They could do nothing. I was **DOOMED**!

"Uh-oh!" she blurted, standing still as a statue.

I wondered what would happen next. Nothing happened! I waited a bit more and more things didn't happen. Then some more nothings.

I prised her fingers open with my tail and gazed up at her frozen face.

Was I **DOOMED***?*

Windy Wendy was strangely rooted to the spot. And her belly was making very odd sounds...

Flurgle-gurgle -swizzle-flizzle- flurrble-glurrble

"What's happening?" she wailed, clutching her rumbly tum. I fell from her giant fumbly fingers...

... and landed on my feet (it's a cat thing).

Everyone in Tattiebogle Town held their noses, apart from Basil the Elephant, who held his trunk. Windy Wendy whooshed into the sky like a rude balloon doing raspberries.

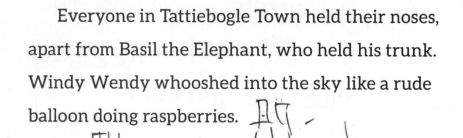

floobb-bloobb-flarttle-blurrpp-fflurrpp-frooble-splib

The trembling Big Yins stared as she twirled over Tattiebogle Town. Higher and higher and further and further she swirled, until all we could see was a wee grubby smudge in the sky.

Soon that was gone, but the nose-watering pong hung about a lot ponger, er, longer.

Would we ever see Windy Wendy again?

No one knew.

Except me.

And I'm not telling.

(Not until you read a book about Dino Dad...)

26

Guess What I Love?

This is the last chapter. I tried to write more but the story was running out. Och, and the ink. I've got just enough left to tell you about today, when everything was back to normal. Mum was experimenting in the kitchen again.

"I was going to make us toad in the hole," she told the twins. "But I can't find a recipe."

"You just need some toads," giggled Isla.

"And holes," laughed Ross.

Dad walked into the kitchen, carrying a spade. "No more holes, please. I've dug twenty today."

"You should borrow my Shovel-o-Tronic digger," said Grandad, who was sitting at the table, fixing Mum's food mixer... again. It got in a terrible spin when Mum tried making rock cakes, with, er, real rocks.

 Me-oops

"Why don't you make tattie scones?" trilled Gran. "I always do."

"Stay back, everyone. I know what I'm doing," said Mini Mum, with a confident grin. She put on her goggles and picked up a fizzing test tube. I dived into my basket and put a furball in each ear.

"Today, we're having bangers and mash for dinner, with extra **BANG!**"

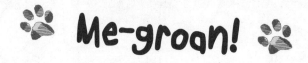 **Me-groan!**

I'd rather have some fresh fishy biscuits, with extra **FISHY BISCUITS!**

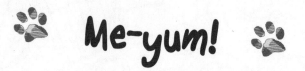 **Me-yum!**

 **I LOVE FISHY BISCUITS!**